I0538749

# Ethan the Eagle and Friends

## Short Stories, Fuzzy Animals, and Life Lessons

Norma MacDonald

*Karma for Kids Books*

Ethan the Eagle and Friends
*Short Stories, Fuzzy Animals, and Life Lessons*

**Copyright © 2016** Norma MacDonald

*First Edition*

Published by: Find Your Way Publishing, Inc.
PO BOX 667
Norway, ME  04268 U.S.A.
www.findyourwaypublishing.com

ISBN-13:  978-0-9849322-8-3

ISBN-10: 0-9849322-8-3

Library of Congress Control Number: 2016937599

Printed in the United States of America.

# Dedication

This book is dedicated to all of the people trying to make the world a better place. You are making a positive difference!

*"You REAP what You SOW: Life is like a boomerang. Our thoughts, deeds and words return to us sooner or later, with astounding accuracy." ~ Grant M. Bright*

# Table of Contents

# About This Book

Welcome to our Karma for Kids Books Series. We are very grateful that you picked up this book. We believe together we can make a positive difference, one child at a time. We strive to instill important life lessons in the lives of young children. We are firm believers in Karma and think that if this simple Law of the Universe is taught to children at a young age, their lives will have the potential to be absolutely amazing.

We once knew a dog named Karma. She was a beautiful, yellow Labrador retriever. It wasn't until after she passed, at 11 years old (God bless her loyal soul.), that we realized just how fitting her name really was.

Karma is indeed a retriever.

Whatever we threw out, Karma was always happy to bring it back to us. It didn't matter what it was, she always brought it back. If we threw out garbage, she'd bring it back without question. If we threw out the most beautiful dog toy, she'd bring it back. It's the same in life. Whatever you send out, is what you will get back. Guaranteed. Every time. Our Karma for Kids Book Series hopes to instill this easy-to-understand Law of the Universe into the lives of children at a young age. The Universe wants to happily bring you all that your heart desires, and it will, effortlessly. But first, you've got to throw out what you want it to bring back to you so that it can! Have fun with this and watch the magic happen. God bless!

Find all of Norma MacDonald's Karma for Kids Books at Amazon.com.

For more of our Karma for Kids books please visit us at:

www.karmaforkidsbooks.wordpress.com
or
www.findyourwaypublishing.com

**Other books that we recommend to help children learn important life lessons:**

*Ethan Eagle and Friends: Short Stories, Fuzzy Animals, and Life Lessons* by Norma MacDonald

*Billy Brown Bear and Friends: Short Stories, Fuzzy Animals, and Life Lessons* by Norma MacDonald

*Humble Heron and Friends: Short Stories, Fuzzy Animals, and Life Lessons* by Norma MacDonald

*Peter Penguin and Friends: Short Stories, Fuzzy Animals and Life Lessons* by Norma MacDonald

*Guaranteed Success for Kindergarten; 50 Easy Things You Can Do Today!* by Marrae Kimball

*Guaranteed Success for Grade School; 50 Easy Things You Can Do Today!* by Marrae Kimball

*The Secret Combination to Middle School: Real Advice from Real Kids, Ideas for Success, and Much More!* by Marrae Kimball

Thank you!

# Ethan the Eagle and Friends

Short Stories, Fuzzy Animals, and Life Lessons

Norma MacDonald

*Karma for Kids Books*

NORMA MACDONALD

Chapter One

# Don't Give Up

ETHAN THE EAGLE, flew high over his emerald green island home. His long wings barely moved as he soared high over the hills. The sky above was as blue as the crystal clear waters that surrounded the white and orange sand beaches. Smoke blew out of the top of Marapi, the island's most active volcano. But something was wrong. Fire and smoke also seemed to be moving quickly into the forest. Wildfire!

Ethan flew quickly away from the smoke. His eyes burned as he headed toward home where his family had built their nest at the top of the tallest pine tree. Had any of the other animals seen the fire? Had anyone sounded the alarm? Ethan flew as fast as his wings would carry him. He needed to warn the Sumatran Forest animals before it was too late.

As he neared his treetop nest, the lush green forest below bustled with activity. Ethan spotted many of his friends—Matthew the Monkey, Sammy the Sun Bear, Terry the Tiger, and Elaine the Elephant. Ever since the big rains ended the month before, all the animals of Sumatra were busy, busy, busy. Except for one. Ethan swooped down to talk with Randy the Rhinoceros as he cooled off lazily in the river. Ethan tried to tell him about the fire, but he didn't seem concerned. "No worries," he said.

"You probably just imagined the fire. I'm safe here in the water already anyway. No worries."

Two of the Orangutans, the big orange apes, moved through the trees next to the river. Ethan waved and waved with his wings, but the orangutans ignored him. He couldn't get their attention no matter how hard he tried. Most animals knew that the orangutans liked to be left alone, but Ethan had hoped this time would be different. It wasn't.

Maybe Linda the Leopard could help him sound the alarm about the fire. He searched through the trees and found her sleeping on her favorite branch. "Wake up!" he shouted.

Linda opened one eye. "Can't you see I'm busy sleeping," she grumbled. "Let me be." She closed her eye and within a few seconds began to snore. Leopards liked to sleep a lot. He didn't dare wake her up again. He knew she'd be very grumpy and growly if he did. So he went off as fast as he could to find someone else.

Ethan flew up above the trees to try to spot his other friends again, but they'd all disappeared into the dense forest. Ethan started to worry. The animals needed to know about the fire danger. What could he do?

Finally, Ethan saw a large group of deer. Surely they would sound the fire alarm. He flew down and landed on a branch just above them. "Hey there! There's a fire on the edge of the forest near Marapi the Volcano. Will you please sound the alarm?"

"Are you sure it wasn't just smoke from the volcano?" asked David, the oldest of the Deer. "The volcano has been erupting for several days. The air is full of smoke."

"No," said Ethan. "It's a wildfire. I'm certain of it."

"Has anyone else seen the fire or smelled the smoke?" asked David. "We don't want to sound a false alarm."

"I don't know if anyone else has seen it," said Ethan. "But it's coming fast and we need to get to safety!"

"Unless we know for sure there's really a fire," said David. "We're not going to send all the animals into a panic."

Why didn't anyone believe him? Wildfires were a huge danger. Somehow he needed to convince them he could be trusted, that he was telling the truth. "Please," he begged. "I know what I saw and it's coming our way!"

"Sorry," said David. "We're not going to sound the alarm if you're the only one who's seen the fire. No one else has said one thing about it. Maybe your eyes tricked you."

"But I have super good eyes. I know what I saw," said Ethan, his voice showing his frustration.

But the Deer wouldn't listen. In the meantime, the fire grew bigger and bigger and moved closer and closer. Ethan flew back and forth over the forest and tried to warn everyone that the fire was coming, but no one listened.

The orange sun began to dip down into the blue sea and air grew cooler. Ethan didn't know what else he could do. He'd almost given up when Freddy, the Flying Fox Bat, flew past him. "Hey, wait up!" said Ethan as he caught up to the bat and flew beside him. "Where are you going in such a hurry? I need to talk to you. It's important."

"I'm hungry. I'm searching for a good patch of eucalyptus trees. I hear there are lots of yummy blossoms right now," said Freddy. Flying fox bats loved to eat eucalyptus flowers.

"I know you must be starving and I would help you find the trees, but there's a fire burning towards us and the Deer don't trust me. They refused to sound the alarm unless someone else sees the fire besides me. No one believes me."

"A fire?" asked Freddy. "Where?"

"Follow me," said Ethan with relief. Finally, someone believed him. The two of them flew east toward Merapi the Volcano. Smoke filled the air and the branches crackled as the big trees burned.

The fire moved closer and closer to the area where the animals lived. Ethan and Freddy flew as fast as they could back to their forest home and found the Deer. When they heard the news from both the Ethan, the Eagle and Freddy the Flying Fox Bat, they sounded the alarm right away.

Immediately, the forest animals raced to safety. The orangutans and monkeys, the sun bears and tigers, and the deer all ran to get to the other side of the wide river. The elephants and rhinos waded into the water, knowing they'd be safe there. The birds and bats flew to the tallest trees on the other side of the river and watched as the flames ate up many of the trees and plants and flowers. The fire crackled and burned, but as soon as it reached the river, it could go no further, turned away, and finally burnt out. The animals were safe!

The next day a large group gathered at the edge of the river and stared out at the empty black forest that had been their home just a day before. It was a close call. They wondered who saw the fire first and why someone hadn't sounded the alarm earlier.

"I tried to let everyone know as soon as I saw the fire," explained Ethan. "But all of you seemed too busy doing something else to listen or else you didn't believe me."

Randy the Rhinoceros, the orangutans, Linda the Leopard, and David the Deer all apologized to Ethan the Eagle. "We're sorry we didn't believe you."

From that day on, all the animals of the Sumatran Forest decided it was best to listen and believe whenever someone warned them of danger, especially smoke and fire. Ethan the Eagle felt good that he hadn't given up in telling others about the fire. Many of the animals' lives were saved because of his persistence.

Chapter Two

# Grandmother Tiger Needs Help

HAPPY BIRDSONG AND the chatter of monkeys filled the warm mountain air each morning in the emerald forest of Sumatra. It was a happy place. Plenty of food and shelter for everyone.

Porcupines scooted beneath the trees digging for roots for their breakfast. The Orangutans searched the trees for their favorite food--durian. This fruit looked spiky on the outside and smelled stinky, but was creamy on the inside and tasted like custard.

The elephants spent most of their time munching on grasses and plants and bushes and twigs. Elephants had big appetites and needed to eat lots of food every day. Sun bears had it the easiest. They could eat all sorts of things like fruit and nuts and berries, but sometimes they also ate ants and other bugs. Like most bears, their favorite treat was golden sweet honey. The tigers were the big hunters. They had to work the hardest to get their food.

By the end of the morning, most of the young animals in the Sumatran Forest had filled their bellies and looked for something fun to do. On that day, Randy the Rhino thought it would be fun to play hide and seek. The rest of the animals agreed. Since it was Randy's idea, the group decided that everyone else would hide and Randy would be the one to find them.

Paula the Porcupine searched for the best place to hide and found a perfect spot under a large fig tree. She soon saw Randy the Rhino tromping down the path nearby. She tried to be very, very quiet and not move a single quill on her prickly body. But then a soft groan came from somewhere nearby. "If only I had someone to help me," the voice said.

Paula didn't want to be found, so she didn't say anything. She waited quietly until the rhino had gotten far enough away. Then she heard the voice again, so she whispered, "Who's there?"

"Sandy."

Paula the Porcupine recognized the name. It was Grandmother Tiger. Her voice sounded very weak. "What's wrong? Why are you groaning?" asked Paula.

"I'm hungry, but I've hurt my leg and can't go hunting for food. Can you help me?" asked the old tiger.

The porcupine didn't know what to say. Surely Grandma Tiger knew that porcupines couldn't hunt food. Plus, Paula didn't want to leave her hiding spot and risk getting spotted by Randy the Rhino. She hated to lose at games. So Paula said, "I'm sorry. But I can't do anything for you."

A few minutes later Paula heard the home free signal and scurried back down the path to meet the other animals. During the next game of hide and seek, Elaine the Elephant had a hard time finding a place to hide. Even though she was small compared to most elephants, it was still really difficult to hide her big body. She finally found a spot in a giant bush near the fig tree where Paula the Porcupine had been hiding during the last round. Sandy, Grandmother Tiger, called out again. "Please. Can someone get something for me to eat?"

Elaine recognized Grandmother Tiger's voice, but she was afraid it might be a trap. She'd heard that sometimes tigers attacked young, small elephants. So she pretended that she didn't hear her.

During the next round of hide and seek, it was Sammy the Sun Bear who hid near the tree where Grandmother the Tiger was resting. When she cried out again asking for food, Sammy answered. "What's wrong, Grandmother? Why can't you go hunting?"

"I've hurt my leg and can't run. I can barely walk. Can you help me?" asked Sandy the Tiger.

Sammy the Sun Bear thought about it for a moment. Something had to be done to help Grandmother Tiger. Sun bears weren't hunters, but there was one kind of food that might make the tiger happy. "Let me go find my friends and we'll bring you back something special as soon as we can."

Sammy the Sun Bear called out in a loud voice on the way back down the path. "Come out. Come out everyone. We have something very important to do."

Within a few minutes, all the young animals appeared and gathered around Sammy. "What's going on? What's so important?" they asked.

Sammy explained about Grandmother Tiger. "If we all go to the big river, maybe we can catch enough fish so that Sandy won't be hungry anymore."

The group cheered. Fishing was so fun! But as they hurried to the river, Paula the Porcupine and Elaine the Elephant lowered their heads and walked slowly. They realized they should have done something to help Grandmother Tiger instead of being selfish and scared.

Sammy the Sun Bear noticed Paula and Elaine's sad faces. "What's wrong? Don't you want to catch fish for Grandmother Tiger?"

"We're happy to go fishing, but we're sad because earlier we ignored Sandy when she asked us to help her," Paula and Elaine explained. "We wish we'd been brave and caring like you."

"We all make mistakes," said Sammy the Sun Bear. "But the important thing is that you can be a *big* help now."

And they were. The animals tried their best to catch a whole bunch of fish so Grandmother Tiger wouldn't starve. They laughed as they splashed in the water, working hard together but having lots of fun, too. Within an hour, they caught more than enough fish to feed Grandmother Tiger. The animals joyfully carried the slippery fish up the path and made a big pile next to Grandmother Tiger. When she saw all that they had brought, her eyes filled with tears of joy. "Thank you, children. I don't know what I would have done without your help."

The young animals of the emerald Sumatran Forest left Grandmother Tiger with enough food for her to eat for a week and promised to go fishing for her again anytime she needed, while her leg healed. With joyful hearts, the young animals skipped down the path and chattered cheerfully about how much fun they'd had fishing for Grandmother Tiger. Helping an older animal made them so happy.

## Chapter Three

# A Nap or Not

THE HOT SUN MOVED lazily across the sky in the Sumatran Forest and by late afternoon the air felt like a heavy blanket. Many of the animals liked to find a comfortable spot in the cool shade of a large tree. There they would take nice long afternoon naps.

But Matthew the Monkey hated to take naps. He wanted to play instead. So he swung from branch to branch and tree to tree, searching for a playmate. Before long, Matthew spotted Gita the Orangutan sleeping under a palm tree. "Wake up!" he said and clapped his hands. "Let's go!"

Gita the Orangutan, opened her eyes. "What's wrong? Is there an emergency?" she asked.

"Do you wanna come play with me?" asked Matthew.

Gita shook her head. "No. I don't want to play. Couldn't you tell I was sound asleep? Please leave me alone." She turned her back to Matthew and went back to sleep.

*What a grouch* thought Matthew as he went off to find someone else. He found Terry the Tiger resting high up on a wide tree limb. His tail hung down beneath him. Matthew yanked on his tail. "How about a game of chase? Betcha can't catch me."

"If I catch you, I'll eat you," Terry growled. "Why did you interrupt my afternoon rest?"

Matthew scampered away from the angry tiger and continued his search for a playmate. He found Randy the Rhino relaxing in the cool water of the river.

"Hey!" shouted Matthew. "Do you wanna race me to the other side. I bet I can swim faster than you."

Randy's big body lowered deeper into the water. Matthew could only see the Rhino's eyes and those eyes didn't look happy. Matthew grunted. He was certain that Randy didn't want to lose. That's why the rhino wouldn't race. Matthew didn't really like to swim anyway. So off he went to find someone else to play with.

A little further into the forest, Matthew saw a group of deer huddled in a circle. He bounced down from the tree above and landed right in the middle of them. "Are you playing a game?" he asked as he bounced up and down. "Can I play, too? Can I?"

The deer stomped their hooves on the ground. "We are having an important discussion which you just interrupted, Matthew. Where are your manners?"

"What important thing are you talking about?" asked Matthew. "Are you planning a party? Can I come?"

"It's really none of your business," barked one of the deer. "Now go find something else to do."

Matthew pouted. Why was everyone acting so rude? He just wanted to have some fun. Didn't any of the other animals understand that?

For another hour, Matthew searched for a playmate. He asked the orangutans, the porcupines, the sun bears, the tigers, the leopards, the rhinos, the deer and the elephants. But no one wanted to play with him.

Matthew couldn't figure out why all the animals were so grumpy and being so mean to him. Feeling sad and angry, he found his favorite banana tree. He grabbed a bunch of bananas and thought about how all the other animals had been rude to him. While he was eating his second banana, Freddy the Flying Fox Bat landed on a branch nearby. "What are you up to?" he asked.

But Matthew didn't answer. He just kept eating his banana.

Freddy swooped down closer. "Didn't you hear me?"

Matthew opened his mouth, which was full of banana, and said, "I'm busy eating. What do you want?"

"Aren't you going to offer me one of those bananas?" asked the bat.

"Get your own bananas," said Matthew. Everyone had been rude to him, so he thought he'd do the same.

But Freddy the Flying Fox Bat was shocked by Matthew's rudeness. "What's wrong, Matthew? Are you upset about something?"

Matthew swallowed the rest of his banana and lowered his head. "No one wants to play with me," he muttered.

Freddy hung upside down from the branch right above Matthew's head and looked him straight in the eyes. "Why do you think no one wanted to play with you?"

"Cause they're all mean," he said.

The bat blinked a few times and thought about how to respond. "Maybe they weren't being mean," he said. "Maybe they were just busy doing something else."

"Too busy napping," said Matthew. "They didn't have to get mad at me just because I woke them up. Why does everyone have to rest so much anyway?"

Freddy sighed. "Matthew, not everyone is like you, loaded with energy. You need to try to be considerate of other animal's needs."

Matthew scratched his head. "What's considerate mean?"

"It means you think about what others want and need. You wanted to play this afternoon, but the other animals needed to sleep. If you woke them up, you weren't being rude and not considerate."

"Is that why they got angry?" asked Matthew.

"I'm sure it had something to do with it," said Freddy.

Matthew scratched his head again. "So being considerate means not waking your friends up when they're sleeping, right?"

"Right," said Freddy. "And another way to be considerate is to offer to share your bananas with your friends when they don't have any."

Matthew handed Freddy a piece of banana. "Here. I wasn't being considerate to you."

"Thank you," said the bat. "Can you think of any other ways you can be caring and thoughtful with your friends?"

"Hmm," said Matthew. "Is telling people you're sorry a way to be considerate?"

Freddy smiled. "Definitely."

Matthew climbed up to the limb next to Freddy. "Then I'd better get going. I have a lot of friends I need to say I'm sorry to."

And so Matthew went back and visited all the animals he'd spoken to earlier that day—the orangutans, the porcupines, the sun bears, the tigers, the leopards, the rhinos, the deer and the elephants He told each one of them how sorry he was for waking them up, for interrupting, and for being rude. From that day on, he would try hard to remember to be more considerate of others.

The next day he would attempt to find someone to play with in the morning time when they weren't resting or busy doing other things. Even though Matthew never did find anyone to play with that afternoon, he went home feeling good in his heart.

Chapter Four

# She's Late Again?

LIFE IN THE SUMATRAN Forest moved along the way it did in most every other forest around the earth. Everything happened at a certain time. The sun rose over the emerald green hills in the misty mornings and dipped into the crystal blue ocean in the evenings. There was a time to eat and a time to sleep. A time to work and a time to play. When all the work was done, the young animals often made plans to go exploring and have various adventures. Most afternoons someone would decide on a time and place to meet and from that spot they'd choose one of the many directions they could explore. Most of the animals arrived at the starting point when they were supposed to, right on time. But one of the animals was almost always late.

Linda the Leopard looked up at the sun high in the sky. "It's already past noon. How much longer should we wait for Paula?" she asked.

"Maybe she's not coming," said Elaine the Elephant. "I haven't seen her this morning."

"She's always late," said Terry the Tiger. "I say we leave without her this time."

The group agreed. They'd already been waiting more than half an hour, so they decided to go exploring up in the green hills without their spiky little friend.

In the meantime, Paula the Porcupine shuffled up the path as fast as she could go. Out of breath, she reached the top of the path, waddled into the clearing, and looked around. Where was everyone? Maybe they were playing hide and seek or something. She walked toward the closest group of tall trees. "Hey! I'm here. You can come out now," she shouted.

But no one answered. Had they left without her? They knew she was coming. What was she going to do by herself all afternoon? Paula found a spot in the shade and pouted. It wasn't fair. She'd lost track of time while cleaning up her room. Now she had to spend the afternoon all by herself with nothing to do.

A little while later, Paula's uncle came up the path and approached her. "What are you doing up here all by yourself?" he asked.

"My friends left without me," she said and stuck out her bottom lip.

Her uncle gave her a stern look. "Were you late again?"

"A little," Paula mumbled.

"Hmm. If they left without you, I suspect you were more than a little late. How many times have you been told, Paula, that a late arrival is a rude arrival?"

"But it wasn't my fault," Paula cried.

Her uncle shook his head. "I've heard those words from your mouth far too many times. I'd like to help you, my dear niece, but you're going to have to cooperate."

Paula sniffed. "What can I do?"

"First of all, you can get up and walk with me or I'm going to be late, too. We can talk about it on our way home."

And so the two of them moved down the path together. Paula's uncle gave her several suggestions of how she might make some changes so that she could be on time. He talked about getting up out of bed first thing in the morning. "Do you have a hard time with that?" he asked.

Paula nodded. Then her uncle talked about the need to stop what she was doing when she knew it was time to leave.

"But what if I'm supposed to clean up and I'm not done when it's time to go?" she asked. "That's what happened today."

Paula's uncle scratched his head. "It's a matter of being organized. If you had gotten up earlier, you would have had plenty of time to clean, right?"

"I suppose you're right. But I still don't understand why my friends didn't wait for me. They knew I was coming. You said a late arrival is a rude arrival but wasn't it rude for them to leave without me?"

"I think we're getting to the root of the problem," Uncle said. He went on to explain about attitude. He asked Paula how she felt about being late.

"I don't think it's a big deal," she said. "Everyone's late sometimes."

"That's true," said Uncle. "But not everyone is late all the time. It's a matter of manners."

Paula scratched her nose. "But I have good manners. I say 'please' and 'thank you' and 'excuse me' all the time."

Uncle patted her head. "Yes, dear. You are very polite and that's wonderful. But each time you show up late, you make everyone else wait for you, and that is not polite. It's very bad manners, and very disrespectful." Uncle looked up at the sky. "Oh my, it's really getting late. Your auntie will be quite upset with me if I'm not home for supper when it's ready."

Paula agreed. "My mother told me if I'm late for supper one more time, she'll send me to bed without any."

"Well then, you'd better hurry along, too. I trust that the next time I see you, you'll be right on time."

"Thank you, Uncle," said Paula, before she headed toward home. As she hurried down the path, she thought about all the things her uncle had told her. She didn't want to be a rude person. She began to understand why her friends were often mad at her. And why her parents got angry, too.

Paula the Porcupine decided she would make whatever changes needed in order to be on time from that day forward. For sure it would take some good planning, and self-discipline, but she knew she could do it. Every morning she would try to be the first one out of bed. She'd get ready for the day and get her work done quickly. She would manage her time and always try to leave five minutes early. Then she'd never have to worry about being left behind by her friends. She would never have to miss out on a fun adventure again.

Chapter Five

# Where Does Courage Come From?

SAMMY THE SUN BEAR woke up in the middle of the night with a special hunger in his belly. That hunger could only be satisfied with one thing—honey. So Sammy quietly got up, tiptoed past his sleeping parents, and carefully dipped one paw all the way to the bottom of the honey jar. Without making any noise, he licked and licked and licked all that golden sweetness until he'd cleaned his paw completely. Sammy went back to bed happy and satisfied.

First thing in the morning, he yawned and rubbed his eyes. His mother stood over him with her arms crossed. "Did you sneak into the honey jar last night?" she asked.

Sammy knew it was wrong to lie, but he also knew if he admitted what he'd done, his mother wouldn't let him go on the big adventure the young animals had planned for that day. He was afraid to admit what he'd done, so he shook his head "no". He quickly got up out of bed and scurried out of the den. He didn't feel good about himself, but he tried not to think about it. Instead, he put his mind on the fun day ahead. A day at the beach!

All the young animals arrived right on time, including Paula the Porcupine. The walk to the beach would take two hours through a very thick jungle. The animals had to be very careful because there were dangers in that jungle. The biggest danger came from the poisonous tree viper. A big snake with a mean bite. The animals knew they needed to stay on the path and make lots of noise so they wouldn't startle those grumpy snakes.

Elaine the Elephant and Randy the Rhino led the way, followed by Linda the Leopard, Matthew the Monkey, and Terry the Tiger. Ethan the Eagle and Freddy the Flying Fox Bat followed in the air and kept an eye out for any other dangers along the path.

Sammy the Sun Bear stayed at the back of the pack with his friend, Paula the Porcupine, who moved a bit slower than all the other animals. As they walked along, Paula liked to stop every once in a while when she found a tasty treat, like her favorite root or a patch of her favorite berries. Sammy was always on the lookout for a beehive. Where there were bees, there was honey!

Before long the two friends had fallen way behind the others. They were so busy talking, and laughing, and collecting snacks, they didn't notice they were being followed by a pack of wild dogs. It wasn't until they reached a clearing to stop and eat their snacks that they realized they had a big problem.

One of the biggest of the wild dogs, Dhole, bounded up to Paula the Porcupine. "Give me all your food!" he demanded.

Paula shrunk back in fear. Sammy the Sun Bear wasn't any help. If there was one thing he feared more than anything, it was wild dogs. He wanted to help his friend, but he was too afraid to speak up. Instead, he climbed up the nearest tree and closed his eyes.

Paula's whole body shook. Her quills quivered. "Leave me alone," she said, her voice a weak little squeak.

"What are you going to do about it, Spiky? Throw one of your tiny needles at me? You couldn't hit me with one of those things if I was standing right in front of your nose!"

From his spot in the tree, Sammy the Sun Bear opened one eye to see what was happening. As he watched, Dhole the Wild Dog stole all the food that Paula the Porcupine had gathered. Then Dhole and the pack of wild dogs ran away, laughing.

Sammy the Sun Bear came down out of the tree and found Paula sitting under a fig tree sobbing. Sammy tried to comfort her, but she wouldn't let him. "Why didn't you help me?" she asked.

Sammy the Sun Bear didn't have an answer. He was afraid to admit that he was scared. He knew he should have helped his friend, even if he was frightened by the wild dogs. Paula the Porcupine continued to sniffle as the two of them walked the rest of the way to the beach in silence. For the second time that day, Sammy felt a big sadness in his heart.

When they got to the beach, all their friends were already there. Elaine the Elephant and Randy the Rhinoceros played in the ocean while Matthew the Monkey and the others built sand houses with tunnels connecting with each other. Paula the Porcupine and Sammy the Sun Bear joined in the sand house building. They were all having a great time when Elaine the Elephant pointed out to sea and shouted. "Hey! Look at that!"

A group of dolphins played in the ocean just a little way from the shore. Sammy couldn't see very well, so he stood up on his hind legs to get a better look. He stood still for a long time and didn't realize all the other animals were staring at him. "What?" he asked.

Matthew the Monkey began to laugh. "Sitting up like that you look like one of the orangutans."

Sammy felt embarrassed and immediately got back down on all four paws like all the other animals. He didn't like to stand out as different from everyone else. A little while later, Sammy sat down by himself and watched his friends playing in the water. They laughed and squirted each other with water. "Sammy, are you coming?" asked Elaine the Elephant.

Sammy wanted to join them, but he was afraid a big wave might come and wash him out to sea. "I'll just stay right here where it's safe," he said.

Some of the animals teased him, but his good friend Elaine the Elephant understood. Elaine got a trunk full of water from the sea and then came and sprayed it all over Sammy the Sun Bear. The cool water felt great and they had a good laugh. But Sammy continued to feel sad.

"What's wrong?" asked Elaine the Elephant. "Do you want to talk?"

The two of them went to talk alone amongst a grove of palm trees. Sammy the Sun Bear explained why he was feeling sad. First, he had been scared to tell his mother the truth about dipping in the honey pot, then he'd been afraid to help his friend Paula the Porcupine when she was being bullied by the wild dogs, and now he was too scared to go play in the water with everyone else. "What can I do?" asked Sammy.

Elaine the Elephant thought about it for a few minutes and then gave an answer. "You need to find some courage," she said.

Sammy looked puzzled. "Where am I supposed to look for courage?"

Elaine touched the end of her trunk to her friend's chest. "Right inside here."

"Really?" Sammy stared down at his chest. "It's inside me?"

"It is. You just need to let it come out."

On the way back home, Sammy thought about what he'd do when he got home. He'd see if he really could let his courage come out by confessing to his mother that he'd dipped into the honey pot. But first, he needed to find the courage to apologize to Paula the Porcupine for not helping her when the wild dogs bullied her. He took a deep breath and went to find his friend, confident that his courage would come out.

"Paula, I'm sorry I didn't help you earlier today. I got nervous and didn't know what to do", he felt uncomfortable and nervous but continued counting on the courage he had within himself to get through it because he knew it was the right thing to do. "If that ever happens again, I will be sure to be courageous and stand up for you. Do you forgive me?"

"I forgive you," Paula gave Sammy a hug.

This courage thing really is within.

Later that day, Sammy told his mom the truth about the honey pot, and she forgave him too.

As for his fear of the ocean waves, it was now dark so he'd have to save that bit of courage for another day.

## Chapter Six

# The Missing Package

ONCE A YEAR, all the elephants from all over the island of Sumatra made a special journey to gather together at Lake Toba. There they'd spend a week on the shores of the huge lake reuniting and visiting with all the herd. When the special day arrived, the young elephants bounced around with excitement. The week would include seeing old friends and eating special food and playing lots of games together.

That morning, Elaine the Elephant smiled a big, proud smile. She'd been given the important job of carrying a special gift to give to her grandparents. For months, they'd been collecting carrots and sugar cane and other special treats for them. The package was big and heavy, but Elaine felt happy to be the one to bring it.

The dozen or so elephants from Elaine's village set out early in the morning, just as the sun was coming up and mist filled the forest. The air smelled fresh and fragrant as the birds sang their loud morning songs. The journey would take an entire day, but the elephant families would stop frequently to rest and relax along the way.

Elaine walked in the middle of the herd. The gift weighed heavy on her back, but she didn't care. As she walked along, she imagined the joy on the faces of her grandparents-- their big, happy smiles. She couldn't wait to see them.

After a couple hours of walking up the narrow path, the elephants wound their way over to the big river. They stopped to have a drink and play in the water. Elaine didn't want her grandparents special package to get wet, so she removed it from her back and put in a safe place under a large fig tree.

Elaine and her young elephant friends splashed in the water. They filled their trunks and sprayed each other, laughing and laughing. The cool water felt so good after the hot hiking on the trail. When her father raised his trunk in the air and sounded the signal for them to go, Elaine and her friends took their time joining the herd. They were having too much fun.

Fifteen minutes later, Elaine's mother moved to the back of the herd to talk to her. "What did you do with your grandparent's present?" she asked.

"Oh no!" Elaine realized she'd make a terrible mistake. She'd left her grandparents gift under the fig tree by the river. "I'll run back and get it right now," she said.

As she ran down the trail, Elaine worried about the package. What if one of the forest animals had found it and taken it? What would she tell her parents? What would she say to her grandparents? She couldn't believe she'd forgotten. How could she be so careless? Tears ran down her face.

When she arrived at the river, she raced straight over to the fig tree. But there was nothing there! She looked all around, using her trunk to move branches and leaves. Nothing. Maybe she was at the wrong tree. Elaine looked all around. But there was only one fig tree and she was certain she'd left it under that one. She searched the area one more time, then fell to the ground and sobbed. The package had disappeared.

Elaine cried and cried and when she could cry no more, she realized her parents would be worried about her. She needed to run back and catch up with the elephant herd before they got too far ahead. But before she could stand up, she heard a voice calling to her from a nearby tree. "Why are you crying?" the voice asked.

Elaine looked up and saw a large tree viper hanging from a branch. She brightened. Maybe the tree viper had seen what happened to the package. So she asked. But the tree viper had been sleeping. He didn't see anything. It was actually Elaine's crying that had woken him up. "But don't give up," said the large tree viper. "Large packages can't walk off by themselves. You'll find it!"

But Elaine didn't think so. She figured one of the rhinos or orangutans had probably found it and taken it home and eaten everything. Her head hung low as she hurried up the path to catch up with the herd. She dreaded telling her parents that the gift was gone.

It took an hour for her to reach the other elephants. She didn't want to talk with anyone, so she stayed to the back of the herd and didn't get too close to the others. She couldn't help but think about how irresponsible she'd been. What would everyone think of her? Would anyone ever trust her with anything again?

After a little while, her closest friend, Tika, came back and walked beside her. "What's wrong?" she asked.

Elaine didn't want to explain about losing the package. Instead, she asked her friend if she'd ever made a big mistake that she wasn't able to fix.

Tika nodded. "I've made lots of them."

"But have you ever lost something really important?" asked Elaine.

"Oh yes," said Tika. "One time my father gave me a bag of special stones and I was supposed to take them to Grandfather Tiger. But I wasn't careful and didn't notice that I'd caught the bag on a branch and tore a hole in the bottom of it. Before I realized, half of the stones had fallen out. I tried to find them all, but there were so many and the ground was covered with dead leaves. It was terrible."

"What did you do?" asked Elaine. "Did you stop searching and tell your father what happened?"

"I didn't give up. In fact, I asked a group of monkeys to help search with me. I promised to give them a bunch of bananas for each stone they found. They were happy to help."

Elaine thought about what Tika said. Maybe she should have asked for help finding the package. But it was too late. It was gone forever. A tear dripped out of her eye and slid slowly down her large elephant cheek.

"What's wrong?" asked Tika.

Elaine burst out crying again. Between sobs and tears, she explained to her friend Tika about losing the package she was carrying to her grandparents. She told her about going back to find it under the fig tree, where she had left it, but that it was gone. "I haven't told my mother and father yet," she said. "I know they're going to be so disappointed with me. They'll never trust me with anything important ever again."

Tika bounced up and down and got all excited. "Oh. Oh. Oh."

Elaine thought maybe Tika had seen something moving on the ground or something. She looked down but saw nothing. "What's the matter?" she asked her friend.

"I think I know what happened to your package," she said.

"You do?" asked Elaine with hope in her eyes.

Tika nodded. "Wait just a minute. I'll be right back."

Elaine watched as Tika raced up ahead to the front of the herd. She lost sight of her for a little while. But soon enough, Tika came back down the path carrying something on her back. It was Elaine's lost package!

"Where did you find it?" Elaine asked with excitement.

Tika explained that one of the older elephants had seen it under the fig tree and was worried that someone would take it. So the older elephant had picked it up and carried it.

"Thank you so much," said Elaine. "I'm so happy now."

During the rest of the journey, Elaine thought about what had happened and what she could have done differently. She realized she should never have left an important package under a tree by itself. She could have given it to one of the older elephants for safe-keeping while she played in the water. In the future, she would be much more careful.

Tired from the long journey, the elephant herd arrived at Lake Toba just as the sun was starting to set. Elaine found her grandparents and gave them their special gift. They flapped their large ears in appreciation and gave her a big hug with their trunks. All the Sumatran elephants enjoyed a wonderful week relaxing, eating, and playing with all their friends and family.

# AFTERWORD

Thanks again for picking up this book! You are participating in making our world a better place.

For more of our Karma for Kids books please visit us at:

www.karmaforkidsbooks.wordpress.com
or
www.findyourwaypublishing.com

**Find Norma MacDonald and her books online at Amazon.com.**

*Billy Brown Bear and Friends; Short Stories, Fuzzy Animals, and Life Lessons* by Norma MacDonald

*Humble Heron and Friends; Short Stories, Fuzzy Animals, and Life Lessons* by Norma MacDonald

*Peter Penguin and Friends; Short Stories, Fuzzy Animals, and Life Lessons* by Norma MacDonald

## Other books that we recommend to help children learn important life lessons:

*Guaranteed Success for Kindergarten; 50 Easy Things You Can Do Today!* by Marrae Kimball

*Guaranteed Success for Grade School; 50 Easy Things You Can Do Today!* by Marrae Kimball

*The Secret Combination to Middle School: Real Advice from Real Kids, Ideas for Success, and Much More!* by Marrae Kimball

If you have ideas for stories, please feel free to share and send them to:

Melissa Eshleman
Find Your Way Publishing, Inc.
PO Box 667
Norway, ME 04268
Melissa@findyourwaypublishing.com

www.findyourwaypublishing.com

Thank you!